CW00504921

£6.99

CONTENTS

Menu

TOM and JERRY

This book belongs to:

Name: Milly

Age: 7

Address: 10 M's grove Woodford

Green IG8 0BV

FUN IN THE SNOW!

Can you spot 10 differences between these two pictures?

Answers: The 10 differences are: 1. Robin. 2. No Skating Sign. 3. Snowball above Jerry. 4. Tuffy's scarf. 5. Snowball

Written and drawn by Oscar Martin

12

Continued on page 18

CHRISTMAS WORD FUN!

O	L	P	S	A	L	P	H	A	U	D
C	R	A	C	K	E	R	T	R	E	E
A	I	R	B	U	D	E	I	L	V	C
K	B	T	U	S	P	S	N	O	W	O
Y	B	Y	K	B	R	E	S	M	I	R
H	O	L	L	Y	B	N	E	S	N	A
C	N	Z	C	P	I	T	L	R	E	T
E	P	O	H	S	S	I	A	W	D	I
Q	G	I	F	T	A	F	E	S	U	O
A	W	E	D	A	R	R	O	B	I	N
G	D	C	H	R	I	S	T	M	A	S

Can you find all the words in the list, hidden in the grid?

- TINSEL
- STAR
- TREE
- PRESENT
- RIBBON
- GIFT
- Christmas DECORATIONS
- SNOW
- HOLLY
- CRACKER
- PARTY
- ROBIN

15

MAKE YOUR OWN TELESCOPE!

You can keep an eye out for alien spaceships, mice, or pirate ships with this easy to make telescope.

YOU WILL NEED:

Cling film, kitchen paper roll, sticky tape, thin card, paint

1 To make the glass lens for your telescope, take a piece of cling film and cover one end of your roll, then stick it down with sticky tape.

2 Cover the outside of your roll with thin card. You can use coloured card or white card and then paint it. Stick it in place with sticky tape.

3 Add an extra narrow strip at the end of your roll. (The end with the cling film)

4 If you haven't any coloured card, paint your telescope. I used black on mine. The end looks good in yellow or gold.

Make sure you put newspapers down on the table before you paint, or you could end up splashing paint everywhere.

NOW YOU'RE READY TO PLAY!

Can you help Tom spot Jerry and Tuffy?

Continued from page 14

How could I have been so *stupid*?

I should've realised Tom was up to something all along! Tom's right! I'm *way* too big and slow like this!

?!

Who dropped that nice chunk of cheese here? Let me at it! Yummy!

Woahh! This has gotta be one of Tom's rotten tricks!

I *won't* give in to temptation! I *won't...* I *won't...*

Deee-lish!

Continued on page 35

JULY

Summer's here and no wonder Tom's feeling crabby!

AUGUST

In August there's nothing quite like chilling out with an ice cream!

SEPTEMBER

It's back to school in September.

OCTOBER

Woooo! It's Hallowe'en!

NOVEMBER

The leaves aren't the only thing that fall down in November.

DECEMBER

What's in Tom's Christmas stocking?

31

GRAND PRIX

Who's going to win the race? It's up to you to help Tom or Jerry reach the finish line first!

COLOURING FUN!

It's time to get your crayons out and get colouring!

Here they come now! Hee--hee!

Klippety-klop klippety-klop klippety-klop

ya-hiii! ya-hiii!

WOOSH

T'WHACK!

This is gonna be one of those days!

aaaaaahhhh!

KER-ASH!

Call me unreasonable, but I'm getting really sick of cactuses!

SINGALONG!

Help Tom and Jerry finish writing their new songs by picking the right words to go in the spaces!

very

house

Jerry

mouse

We are Tom and _Jerry_
Are we cool? Yeah, _very!!_
I'm a cat and he's a _mouse...._
Tom and Jerry are in the _house!!_!

TOM'S NEW GIRLFRIEND

Welcome to my humble abode, my dear. My house is your house. Your every wish, my heart's desire!

Oh *goodness*, Tom, what an adorable little house. Everything is just so *wonderful*!

Written and drawn by Oscar Martin

Tea time I think. Would you *excuse* me while I go to the kitchen?

But *of course*, my charming little man.

Tom wants me to keep out of the way cos his boring girlfriend's here!

You think you can hide from me in your pathetic little hole? Ha! *No chance* Buster!

This is for trying to ruin my date! Take that!

SCHHHHH! SCHHHH!

Cough! Cough! She's trying to gas me with *perfume*!

SHHHHHHHH SHHHHHHH

Good job I bought this at the jumble sale!

I heard some noises. Is everything okay?

Oh yes, I was just admiring your family photos. *So* charming!

That mad kitty has got to go! I'll have to have a word with Tom and put a stop to this!

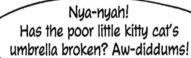

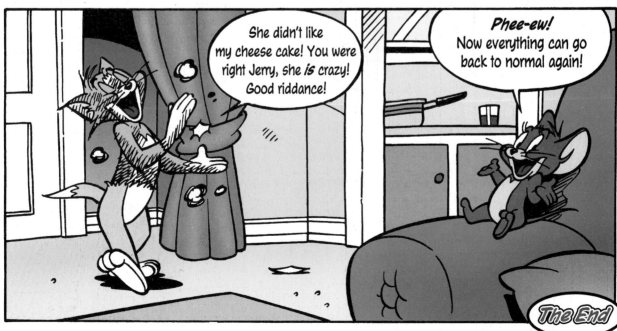

FIND THE PRESENTS!

Get your favourite crayons and colour in the Christmas presents!

game...game...game...g

Can you match all these gifts to the wrapped presents? Which of these gifts hasn't been wrapped?

Answer: Saxophone

?

CLANG

Wha?

you again!

Err...it wasn't me. It was that Dutch Edam cheese!

And you were the one pushing that cheese! I told you to stay in your hole!

Now don't you dare wake me up again, or I'll hang you from the TV aerial by your tail and leave you there for a week!

I hope I've made myself *clear* this time, Jerry?

Yeah...yeah... I'm sorry!

Bah! He's got me so wound up! I bet I won't have *any* sweet dreams now!